This book belongs to:

....

....

 **Quarto** Knows

Quarto is the authority on a wide range of topics.

Quarto educates, entertains and enriches the lives of our readers—enthusiasts and lovers of hands-on living.

www.quartoknows.com

Publisher: Maxime Boucknooghe
Editorial Director: Victoria Garrard
Art Director: Miranda Snow
Designer: Victoria Kimonidou

Copyright © QED Publishing 2016
First published in the UK in 2016 by QED Publishing

Part of The Quarto Group
The Old Brewery
6 Blundell Street
London N7 9BH

A catalogue record for this book is available from the British Library.

ISBN 978 1 78493 796 6

Printed in China

Sleep, Little Pup

Jo Parry

NEW BURLINGTON

At the end of the day,
as the sun starts to set,
as the moon makes
its way to the sky.

As the dark inky shadows stretch out like a cat,
poor Pup, he lets out a sigh.

He tries counting
sheep and gives them
all names, until he can
think of no more.

He counts all the stars that light up the sky,
but nothing will help little Pup snore.

He chases his tail and chews on a bone.

He plays with the mice in the hall.

He rolls like a hedgehog and howls at the moon,
but poor Pup cannot rest at all.

The night shift begins for the beetles and bugs,
as they march from their beds by the log.

The moths and
the fireflies
dance through
the night
and sing
"go to sleep, little dog!"

Hopelessly he tries to slip into sleep,
to drift into magical dreams.

He patrols with the fox through
whispering grass, lit up by
the moon's silver beams.

He skips with the dragonflies down to
the pond, and tickles the fish with his toes.

He floats on the lilies and leaps with the frogs, and ripples the pond with his nose.

As stars paint their light
all over the land, little Pup
looks up at their glow.

As badger

peeps out

from a carpet

of leaves,

he whispers

"to bed you must go."

Nothing he tries brings sleep to his eyes,
nothing will make Pup yawn.

So with a **THUD**
of a paw, he plods across
the floor and returns
to his basket forlorn.

As the clock strikes eleven, Mummy returns, to kiss and cuddle Pup tight.

With a special new blanket, she wraps up her pup
and quietly turns off the light.

The magical blanket so soft and so warm,
is like the loveliest, fluffiest sheep.

It covers little Pup in the happiest warmth
and at last he falls fast asleep.

Next Steps

Show the children the cover again. Could they have guessed what the story is about from looking at the cover?

Ask the children to point to the shadows in the first picture. Help the children to make some shadow puppets on a wall using their hands. Explain that a shadow is made by blocking out the light.

Little Pup meets lots of other animals. Can the children name all the animals that appear in the story? Can they think of any other animals that like to come out at night?

In the story Pup tries many things to make him sleepy. Can the children remember all the things he tries?

Help the children to make twenty sheep by sticking cotton wool onto card. Then stick numbers one to twenty on each sheep, muddle the order, and help the children to arrange the sheep in number order.

At the end of the story, Mummy wraps Little Pup in a new blanket. How do the children think the blanket feels? Ask them to think of some words to describe how Pup feels. Why do they think he finally falls asleep?

Ask the children what they like to do before bedtime. What helps them get to sleep? Do they have a special blanket or toy they like to take to bed?

Ask the children why they think sleep is important for everyone. How do they feel if they haven't had enough sleep?